CLOUDY
with a chance of
MEAT BALLS™ 2

MOVIE NOVELIZATION
ADAPTED BY STACIA DEUTSCH

SIMON AND SCHUSTER

Simon and Schuster
First published in Great Britain in 2013 by Simon & Schuster UK Ltd
1st Floor, 222 Gray's Inn Road, London WC1X 8HB
A CBS Company

Published in the USA in 2013 by Simon Spotlight, an imprint of Simon & Schuster
Children's Division, New York.

A CIP catalogue record for this book is available from the British Library

ISBN 978-1-4711-1836-4
Printed and bound by CPI Group (UK) Ltd, Croydon, CR0 4YY

10 9 8 7 6 5 4 3 2 1

Visit our website: www.simonandschuster.co.uk

Read the original book by
Judi Barrett and Ron Barrett.

CHAPTER 1

Flint Lockwood was reminiscing about his childhood.

"My whole life I've always wanted to be a great inventor. Just like my hero, Chester V!"

Flint remembered how, as a young boy, he would sit in front of his TV set eagerly waiting for his favorite show to come on. And, then, finally, after what seemed like an eternity, there he was—the world's greatest inventor, Chester V!

"Welcome back, Science Friends!" Chester V would say. "Here at Live Corp we are inventing the future, but every dream has a beginning. I still remember my first invention. The humble food bar." Chester held up a photo of himself as a child with his first invention . . . a food bar machine.

"And now look at us," Chester continued. "Still making food bars, still making people happy after all these years. Now kids, you'll almost certainly never be me, but remember, there's no such thing as small science . . . only small scientists! Can your idea change the world?"

Young Flint shouted at his TV set, *"Yes!"*

Flint smiled at the memory as he sat by his computer in his lab. "My dream was to make the world a better place. So I invented this . . ." Flint typed on his keyboard and then pointed at the opening image in the video. "A machine that could turn water into food."

On the screen the machine gurgled, "Cheeseburger!"

"It's called the Flint Lockwood Diatonic Super Mutating Dynamic Food Replicator, or for short, the FLDSMDFR." The video showed Flint pouring water into the top of his creation. A cheeseburger plopped out from the bottom.

Flint scrolled though footage of the day that it rained hamburgers. When ice-cream snow closed schools. The time a candy rainbow arched across the sky.

"Because of my invention's food weather, people

in my town liked me—for the first time in my life!" One of his favorite memories was when he and Sam Sparks, a local weather girl, bounced up and down inside a Jell-O mold. "My machine made everybody happy," Flint said.

He zoomed through the footage, pausing on the night that a gigantic rib-eye steak nearly squashed his father. "Well, almost everybody," Flint admitted.

The video revealed how huge food began crashing down from the sky, crushing famous and important historical monuments.

"Turns out bigger isn't always better," Flint admitted as images of mutant gummi bears and vicious roaster chickens flickered on the screen. "When the storm spread all over the world, and the FLDSMDFR started making dangerous living food, I finally had to face the truth." Flint cringed. His machine had gotten out of control. "It was time to put an end to my FLDSMDFR."

The final shot was of Flint sealing the angry FLDSMDFR with another of his inventions; a can of Spray-On Shoes.

KABOOM! The FLDSMDFR exploded.

Flint pressed a button on the remote and the TV screen went black. "And that is how *we* saved the town that *I* almost destroyed."

Flint shook his head to clear the bad FLDSMDFR memories. "Oh yeah." He smiled. "The point is, by blowing up my greatest invention, I made something even better . . . friends!" Flint looked around happily. He was surrounded by his family, friends, and residents of Swallow Falls.

The crowd cheered.

"You've made me very proud, son." Flint's father, Tim, put his arms around Flint for a bone-crushing hug.

"Thank you, Dad," Flint said.

Flint looked over at Sam Sparks. She was wonderful and pretty and awesome. Sam hadn't just reported the changing weather. She'd helped Flint stop the FLDSMDFR machine.

"Sam Sparks," Flint said. "In the eight minutes since we saved the world, I've had time to reflect, and I think that you and I should have a place together."

Sam's eyes grew huge as if she couldn't believe

what she was hearing. "A place . . . ," she breathed.

"A place where we work," Flint told her.

"You think we . . . work? Together?" Sam asked hesitantly, her eyes glowing with excitement.

Flint nodded. "And maybe . . . we could, maybe, like—work together—forever?"

Sam replied with a dreamy grin. "I do."

Flint was thrilled. "Awwwesome."

He grabbed a piece of paper and began to draw with crayons. "We could build a lab!"

"With cool weather forecasting devices," Sam chimed in.

"What shall we call it?" Flint asked.

"Sparkswood!" Sam shook her fingers like Broadway jazz hands.

"Oooh, Sparkswood." Flint made the same jazz hands. He wrote "Sparkswood" on the paper.

Earl leaned in. "Sparkswood is gonna need some security!" He grabbed the crayon and added himself to the drawing.

Brent drew on the paper next. "And I can be your mascot!" He flapped a roasted chicken wing.

"And I can be your dad." Tim put himself in the corner, then passed the drawing to Manny.

"There are many ways in which I can help," Manny said, adding his own quick sketch.

"Oh! Can't forget you, lab partner!" Flint reached behind him to pick up Steve, his monkey assistant.

"Steve!" Steve said. He spoke through Flint's thought translator invention. The monkey made a mark on the Sparkswood drawing before hopping away.

"This," Flint waved the drawing, "could be our future!"

Sam leaned in to give Flint a kiss, but the kiss was interrupted . . .

CHAPTER 2

A sudden burst of wind blew Flint away from Sam as a fancy helicopter landed in the center of Sardine Circle.

A man with a white beard, glasses, and an orange vest stepped out of the copter, calmly smoothing out his clothes. "Greetings and Namaste."

Sam asked Flint, "Whoa! Is that—?"

Flint couldn't believe his eyes. "Chester V!"

"Mustache!" Steve lunged forward. Flint held Steve back.

"Sorry to barge in like this." Chester waved to the entire town. "Please have some humanitarian aid as a gesture of our good will." His Sentinels of Safety team removed supply boxes from the helicopter and began passing out necessities.

"Food bars!" Earl's son, Cal, cheered.

"Bandages!" Manny took a few.

"Pants!" Joe Towne, one of the oldest citizens of Swallow Falls, said.

Tim took a food bar. He read the label. "Live Corpse? That makes no sense . . ."

Flint took the bar from his father. "No, no, no, Dad, it's *Live Corp*! Rhymes with 'Give More,'" he explained. "Chester V is one of the greatest inventors of all time!"

Chester came up behind Flint.

"Ah! Mr. V . . . I'm a HUGE fan. I have a poster of you over my bed!" Flint was flustered to be in front of his hero.

"So do I." Chester wasn't kidding.

Flint reached out to shake hands, but his hand passed right through Chester. The inventor rippled.

"Whoa! Sorry for that." Flint pulled back. "I must be doing something wrong here." He tried again, and again his hand passed right through Chester.

"There's nothing wrong with your hand, young Lockwood," Chester said. "You see, I am merely a hologram of the real Chester V."

Flint's dad was confused. "If he's a hologram,

why'd he need to take a helicopter?"

Chester explained, "Because, old Lockwood, I used my *Help*-icopter to transport my Thinkquanauts."

Chester's Thinkquanauts bowed their heads and said, "Namaste."

"Eeeee! I've always dreamed of becoming one of Chester's Thinkquanauts." Flint recalled when he was little, back when his mom was still alive. It was Halloween and he was wearing his costume, a home-made orange Thinkquanaut vest. His candy pail was shaped like a laboratory beaker.

Flint's mom was dressed like an angel. She'd forced Tim to be a vampire. He wasn't happy about it.

"Twick or tweat!" young Flint said.

"What is he? A crossing guard?" Tim asked Flint's mom, Fran.

"He's a Thinkquanaut dear," she replied proudly.

"What is that? Some kind of crossing guard?"

Tim had never understood Flint's dreams. But now the Thinkquanauts were in Swallow Falls!

"Awwwesooome," Flint said, checking out their orange vests.

9

"We've come to clean up the leftovers!" Chester told the town. "Our teams are helping everywhere the food storm hit. France, Russia, the Great Wall of China." He quickly flashed through holographic images of the world. The last image was the most familiar. "And of course, your Swallow Falls!"

The crowd burst into applause. "Yay! Woo, Swallow Falls!"

"We'll get started on the cleanup right away. As soon as you all leave," Chester announced with a smile.

The applause stopped.

"What did he say?" an old man asked.

"What? You need us to leave?" Tim stepped toward Chester's hologram.

"Listen up, ghost man!" Earl was steaming mad. "You expect us to skedaddle from our homes just because of some nasty leftovers?"

The Thinkquanauts were busy roping off parts of the island with yellow police tape.

Chester looked at Earl. "Yes. Yes, I do," he said.

"You can't argue with yellow police tape." Earl took off his hat in defeat. "Everybody pack up." He

10

told the crowd, "Listen to ghost man!"

"But do not fret, all of you will be temporarily relocated to sunny San Franjose, California!" Chester announced.

Flint and Sam both gasped. "The home of Live Corp!"

"On my word as a hologram, you shall return home before you know it!" At Chester's promise, the crowd cheered.

"Yay!" Flint said.

"Except for you, Flint Lockwood," Chester said turning his hologram eyes to Flint.

"Me? Really?! Why?" Flint asked anxiously.

"You are going . . ." The Chester hologram suddenly froze with one eye half-open.

"Wait! Where am I going? Please tell me!" Flint was shaking with nerves.

A Thinkquanaut stepped up and said, "Just give it a second. He's buffering."

The hologram loaded and Chester went on. "Because you are going to join me at Live Corp and help me invent a better world for everyone."

11

"That's what I've always wanted," Flint said happily. His nervousness turned to excitement.

"Then work hard," Chester said. "And perhaps someday soon *you* could become—a Thinkquanaut!"

"A Thinkquanaut. Like you." Flint didn't believe what he was hearing. Dreams really could come true.

Sam was thrilled. "Flint! This is a once-in-a-lifetime opportunity!"

Sam drew an orange vest on a sticky note and stuck it on the Sparkswood drawing. Flint's friends gathered around. Sam held up the Sparkswood drawing. "We're all behind you," she said.

"Are you sure?" Flint asked, looking at the art.

"Sure," Sam said with a grin.

The gang gave him a thumbs-up.

Flint rushed over to Chester. "Thank you, Chester V hologram! I accept!"

Flint and his friends were all strapped in to a Live Corp Help-icopter. As it lifted off from the island, they looked out the window.

"My chest hairs are tinglin'," Earl said, glancing over Tim's shoulder to get a last glimpse of the island. "Somethin's wrong."

"Guys, guys, listen. I promise nothing bad will ever happen to us, ever again." Flint felt certain that this was a wonderful new beginning.

As the Helpicopter flew away, one of Chester's holograms pressed a button on his vest. A monitor appeared in front of him, showing the real Chester V.

"Our satellites have confirmed the machine has landed on the island," hologram Chester reported. "The locals have been evacuated."

"Splendid," the real Chester V said. "And the inventor?"

"He took the job. Now we can keep an eye on him," hologram Chester said. "He doesn't suspect we're after his FLDSMDFR."

"Outstanding," the real Chester V. cheered. "Contact me as soon as Operation Capture the Invention succeeds. And hurry! The future of Live Corp depends on it!"

13

The Help-icopter was on its way to San Franjose when the remains of the FLDSMDFR fell from the sky onto the island of Swallow Falls.

It landed in a puddle of water and began to whir to life.

Water entered the top, then filtered through the FLDSMDFR.

A cheeseburger popped out of the bottom. Suddenly the sesame seeds opened, revealing eyes. The cheeseburger was *alive*!

CHAPTER 3

Meanwhile, it was Flint's first day at work in San Franjose. The alarm clock rang at 5:30 a.m.

"Big day! Big day! Big day! Big day! Yes!" Flint rushed around his room, gathering everything he needed. He sprayed on a pair of Spray-On Shoes.

"Wake up, Steve!" Flint shook his monkey friend.

"Steve!" the monkey answered. He eyed Flint and smiled.

"Do I look like a future Thinkquanaut?" Flint asked as Steve popped up, ready for the day.

A curtain in Flint's room swung open. The amazing lab area where Flint slept was in truth just a small corner of a tiny apartment.

"Mornin' there, skipper! You want a sardine scramble?" Tim raised a frying pan.

"No thanks. Can't be late!" Flint headed for the door.

"Catch the big one!" his dad called after him.

Flint groaned. "I don't understand fishing metaphors!"

Sam lived across a narrow, darkened hallway. Flint knocked on her door.

"Morning, Sam!" he said cheerfully.

Sam stepped into the hall while Flint waited for the elevator. "You ready for your first day?"

"Absolutely!" Flint said with a huge grin. "Gotta run! Bye, Sam!" Moving quickly backward, Flint bumped into the elevator door. "Oof," he said as the doors shut.

When Flint got to the bus stop, Manny, Earl, and Brent were already there.

"Well, this is me!" he told his friends when a city bus pulled up. "Good luck with your new jobs, guys!"

"Good luck!" Earl said.

"Break a leg, Flint!" Brent told him.

Flint hung his head out the window. "Byeeeee!"

"Adios!" Manny shouted as the bus pulled away.

16

The bus crossed a bridge to a small island in the San Franjose bay and entered the Live Corp campus. The home of Live Corp was built to look like a giant glowing lightbulb.

"Thanks, Noodle Guy!" Flint told the driver, a pal from Swallow Falls.

"Good luck, Flint."

Flint and Steve headed toward the main entrance. An invisible car pulled up in front of them.

"Wow, Steve!" Flint's head was spinning as he looked around.

They caught an escalator to the main floor where a large orangutan was waiting for them.

"Good morning, Flint Lockwood and friend." She smiled at Steve. "I'm Barb."

Steve looked scared and clung to Flint. "Monkey," he said.

Barb gave Steve an annoyed look. "Excuse me! I'm an ape. One of Chester V's most brilliant innovations. An orangutan with a human brain within my ape brain. Like a turducken. I'll be your welcome ambassador." She handed Flint a cup. "Soy latte?"

Flint took the foamy drink. "Thanks!"

"Are you ready to *live*?" She held up two shiny Live Corp badges.

Flint's eyes widened. "Oh, am I! Sweet!"

Steve bit into his badge. "Plastic," he said.

"Follow me." Barb swiped her badge at a concrete wall and a hidden door materialized. She walked through.

Flint slipped through sideways and gasped, "Wow!"

The spectacular lobby was breathtaking.

Barb led them through the crowd of people. She explained, "There are caffeine stations every ten feet. Gluten free?" She handed Flint another latte.

Flint and Steve followed Barb down the corridor.

"Massage pods and cookie bakery are open twenty-four hours. Our yoga is gravity free, and of course we have a dolphin pool." A dolphin squealed in the background. "Indoor sports are encouraged." She tipped her head to a net where Live Corp employees were playing a game of volleyball.

18

"Cool!" Flint said. "I've never played volleyball."

A noise behind Flint caught his attention. Behind him, several Thinkquanauts wearing orange vests rode by on bubble scooters.

"Thinkquanauts. Awesome!" Flint couldn't take his eyes off them. The Thinkquanauts entered their special orange elevator. "Hey! Excuse me! I'm so looking forward to working with you—" Flint ran after them but the elevator doors shut on his nose. The Thinkquanauts soared up into the private areas of the building.

"That's where we belong, Steve," he told the monkey. "Let's go!"

"Hold on, eager electron. Not until you become a Thinkquanaut." Barb yanked him away from the orange elevator and led him over to the regular tubes on the other side of the room.

"Some of our more determined employees submit one new invention a *month*." Barb pushed Flint into the crowded tube. "So, happy inventing!" she said.

"Thanks. . . . Aaaaaaah!" The tube bottom dropped out and Flint plummeted downward.

19

All around him people dropped from the ceiling. Flint plopped into his work cubicle. The latte cup landed on his desk, empty.

"Yeesh," Flint told Steve. "We'll have to get used to that landing." The liquid from his latte dropped into the cup.

Steve didn't look like he ever wanted to go through that tube again.

Flint said, "Don't worry Steve, in six months we're going to be Thinkquanauts! If the most determined employees are submitting one invention a month, we'll be SUPER determined and submit . . . one invention a *day*!"

"Can!" Steve said, jumping up and down.

"That's the spirit, Steve!" Flint said. "Now let's get another latte and get to work!"

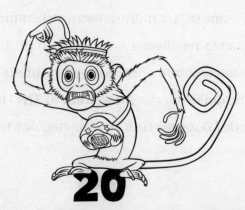

CHAPTER 4

Flint worked hard to create useful inventions.

His first idea was a freeze ray. "Say good-bye to ice cubes with the Re-Freeze-a-Fan!"

Tim held a cup of water. Flint flicked on the freeze ray and turned Tim into a block of ice.

"Fliiiiiint!" Tim said through chattering teeth.

Confident that he was well on his way to becoming a Thinkquanaut, Flint e-mailed the Re-Freeze-a-Fan invention to Chester V for review.

One month later Flint was still working toward achieving his dream.

Sam took the apartment elevator down with him, as she did every day. Sam went to kiss Flint when the elevator door opened.

Flint jumped out with a wave instead of a smooch. "Gotta run! Bye, Sam!"

"Bye!" She smiled as he disappeared down the street.

As Flint hurried to his cubicle, he grabbed a latte out of an employee's hand.

"Thanks!" he shouted as he ran off.

A minute later Flint was busy at work in his cube, no longer bothered by the sheer drop out of the tube. He put on a welding mask and held up a blowtorch.

Ten minutes later he submitted a new invention to Chester V.

Another four months passed.

Flint and Steve continued to come up with brilliant ideas.

Flint hammered, he painted, and he drank a ton of lattes. He stayed at work long after dark until his newest invention was finished.

"Invisible Coffee Table!" Flint said proudly.

Meanwhile, back at home his dad tripped over something invisible in the middle of the apartment. He flopped to the ground, grasping his leg. "Aaah!"

When the fifth month began, Flint was still inventing new things. Energized every day, he rode the elevator down with Sam then hurried off to the bus. "Gotta run! Bye, Sam!"

Every morning Sam wearily watched him go.

One night Flint came home late to discover Tim asleep in his chair. Flint quietly placed a small invention on the table beside him.

"The Celebrationator!" Flint whispered to Steve. "A party in a box for any occasion. Okay Steve, time to celebrate."

"Celebrate!" Steve echoed. The monkey hit the button. The box exploded, splattering the room with glitter, music, and joy.

Tim shot up, awake. "FLIIIIIINT!"

Sam, Earl, Manny, and Brent all popped up from hiding spots in the apartment. "Happy Birthday!"

they shouted. They waited for Tim's reaction.

Tim was freaked out, still sleepy, and confused.

Flint handed Tim a birthday present. "Here you go, Dad! Hope you like it—Steve picked it out." Flint checked his watch. "Well, that was fun! Gotta get back to work. Bye!"

"Bye." Sam watched him leave again.

"Call us," Brent shouted down the hallway.

Flint e-mailed the Celebrationator invention to Chester V. The e-mail was printed out and placed in an overflowing file labeled LOCKWOOD.

Sam stood alone near the elevator. She checked the time.

It was two in the morning. Flint was still at work. Sam sighed. She always knew it was going to be hard to stay in touch with Flint when he was starting out. She just never realized *how* hard.

24

On the day of the six-month deadline, Flint was up extra early. He checked his cell phone and heard a voice mail message left for him from Sam.

"Hi, Flint! It's Sam. I know you've been working like crazy for this. Good luck! Can't wait to see you tonight! I like-like you so much. Bye!"

Upon hearing the message, a huge smile spread across Flint's face. He grabbed the Celebrationator and put it in his pocket. He looked at Steve, grinned, and said, "Orange vest, here we come!"

Flint walked into the Live Corp auditorium beaming with pride. He carried the Celebrationator through the crowd.

Flint instructed Steve, "Okay, Steve. Just like we practiced. When I'm up on stage getting my vest, you hit the red button when I say 'celebrate.'"

"Celebrate!" Steve tried to grab the machine. He was eager to hit the button.

Flint placed his hand over the trigger. "Whoa! Careful, Steve! This is a loaded party in a box! We don't want it going off at the wrong time."

Chester V came out on stage to a thunder of

applause. No one cheered louder than Flint.

"Hello, team Live Corp! It's a pleasure to welcome you to our annual Thinkquanaut Vesting ceremony!"

Flint hooted, "Woo! Chester V!"

On a giant screen the Live Corp mission statement played:

Over an image of Chester in front of Live Corp cutting the ceremonial ribbon, Chester's voice rang out. "I have built the coolest, hippest company in the world! This year I've challenged myself to reinvent taste!"

Images played showing Thinkquanauts passing out food bars.

"Shepherd's pie!" a man said after taking a big bite.

Throughout the world, people reported the different flavors they were trying.

"Schnitzel!"

"Borscht!"

"Tuna fish!"

"Churrascaria!"

A dog took a nibble of a food bar. "Bark!"

Chester came back on the screen. "With so many

flavors, we've invented happiness in a rectangle!"

"Yummmmm!" A group of kids of different nationalities rubbed their bellies.

The video ended and the screen disappeared. The crowd was on their feet, screaming for more. From under the stage, a coveted orange vest rose into view.

"Who will be this year's newest Live Corp Thinkquanaut?!" Chester V asked the crowd.

Spotlights circled the crowd. Flint clapped his hands.

"We have received thousands of invention submissions, and today, one of them can be deemed Thinkquanaut worthy!"

"Yeah!" Flint shouted.

A drum roll began. Barb walked out onstage and handed an envelope to Chester.

"Thank you, Barb," Chester said.

Flint sat up at the edge of his chair.

"This person comes from an island . . ."

Flint leaned forward in his seat.

"He's got a memorable mop of unruly hair . . ."

Steve tugged on Flint's hair, saying, "Hair! Hair!"

27

"Ha-ha! That's me!" Flint told Steve with a wide grin.

"Our newest Live Corp Thinkquanaut is . . . Fliiinnnt . . ." Chester stretched out the name.

Flint stood up, Celebrationator in his hands. "Yeaaaah!"

Chester finished. ". . . ly . . . McCallahan!"

"Nooooo!" Flint couldn't believe his ears.

Flintly McCallahan stood up in front of Flint and cheered!

"Crikey blikey," Flintly said in a New Zealand accent. The man rushed to the stage leaving Flint looking stunned.

Onstage, the screen showed a kitten in a car's gas tank. "For inventing a truly zero-emission car that runs on cute!" Chester said.

"Awwwww!" The audience moaned at the cuteness.

On-screen the kitten purred and the car drove away. It was now branded as the "Live Car."

Flintly received his vest. "This is the greatest day of my life!" he said. "Diggory Doooo! I'm so fulfilled!"

"Sorry, Steve, no reason to celebrate." Flint moaned.

28

Hearing the special word, Steve yelled, "Celebrate!" and hit the button on the Celebrationator.

"Wait, Steve! No, no, no—*nooooo!*" Flint shouted as the box began to shake. Steve jumped back. Flint stuffed the box down the front of his lab coat in a desperate attempt to hide it.

It exploded. The sparkles covered half the auditorium.

When the dust cleared, Flint was dusted in rainbow glitter. The entire crowd erupted in laughter while snapping cell phone pictures and video. *"Hahahaha!"*

A video of the accident was replayed on the jumbo screen onstage. Flint was humiliated.

On the screen Flint could see that Chester had glitter and glue all over his vest. Chester wiped it off, flashing Flint a disappointed look.

The minute Flint was gone, Barb rushed up to Chester V.

"Sir, we've lost contact with cleanup teams X and Y, Barb said.

Chester stared at Barb, panicked. "What?"

"The situation is grim, sir," Barb replied. "Still no sign of the FLDSMDFR. Should I send in team Z?"

"Are you mad, Barb? We'll be all out of alphabet!" Chester shouted. "We're running low on Thinkquanauts, and Live Corp is hanging by a thread as it is. We need someone expendable. Someone who knows the island. Someone smart but naive. Someone who idolizes me but has hit rock bottom and will now do anything I ask of him."

"Where can we find someone that desperate?" Barb asked.

Chester looked around at the smeared paint and glitter in the empty auditorium. He smiled at Barb.

"I think we've already found him," he said.

CHAPTER 5

Flint staggered home, sad and disappointed. The fog was thick. With a sigh, Flint stopped at a shop window. Sam was reporting stormy weather.

He dialed her phone and left a message. "Hi, Sam. It's Flint. I see you're live on TV with a tornado. Probably why you're not answering the phone."

On TV an anchorman introduced a story about the latest viral video. Then the footage cut to an image of Flint's explosion.

"Thinkquanaut?" the anchorman laughed. "I think *not*!"

The replay of Flint's Celebrationator disaster played in slow motion. Underneath, words flashed: THINKQUA-NOT!

Flint swallowed hard. "Please call me back, Sam. Okay. Byeee." He hung up.

When he reached his tiny apartment, Flint flung himself facedown on his bed.

"Flint?" Tim stepped through the curtain between the living room and Flint's laboratory bedroom. He carried a cake shaped like an orange vest. "Whoooo's number one? Ta-daaa." Tim picked a sparkler out of Flint's hair and put it on the cake.

Flint screamed into his pillow.

Tim immediately understood this wasn't a cake moment. He turned awkwardly away.

There was a knock at the front door and Sam came bounding into the apartment. She also carried an orange vest cake.

"Hey, Flint! I got your message." She noticed he was not moving on the bed. "Oh no, what happened to you?"

Flint screamed into his pillow again.

With great effort, Flint managed to get out of bed and dragged himself to the table to eat. He slumped forward, stabbing his cake with a fork. Tim and Sam stared at him.

"Flint, everyone gets humiliated on national

television. It's not that big a deal!" Sam said from personal experience.

"No, Sam, it's worse! I was humiliated in front of Chester V, my childhood hero! I just wanted him to think I was worth something so that I could be a real inventor." Flint dropped his head into his hands.

Steve ate Tim's orange vest cake, and swallowed the sparkler candle. The sparkler made his tail light up.

Flint couldn't take it anymore, and left the room.

Sam followed him, saying, "Flint, you don't need Chester's approval. You can still be a great inventor without a vest."

Flint collapsed onto his mattress. "You guys don't understand. It's not a vest, it's *the* vest."

Sam told Flint, "Is it worth not having a life? It's just a vest, after all. I have to get going. But for what it's worth, I think you look great in your lab coat." She said to Tim, "Goodnight, Mr. Lockwood."

"G'night, my dear." Tim watched her exit, then walked over to the bed and sat down. "Look, Son. This Chester V promised us we'd be home before we know it. Well, we know it. And we're not home. I say

33

you, me, and your friends take the boat. We can go fishing every day and if there's still a mess on the island, we can clean it up ourselves."

Flint sat up. "Dad, please, I'm not into fishing." Flint looked at Tim. "And clean up the island? You're way too old to be doing that kind of work."

"I'm only forty-nine," Tim protested.

Flint shook his head. "Let's face it, Dad. You're past the age of value and I'm a lousy inventor."

Tim was insulted, but before he said anything about it, the doorbell rang. He gave a sorry look at Flint and went to answer the bell. There was an orangutan in the hallway.

"Flint! There's um . . . could you come to the door, please?" Tim gave the ape a sideways look. He then shuffled out of the way, leaving her waiting.

"I think it's that monkey in your poster," Tim said, pointing at the Chester V poster above Flint's bed. Next to the grinning photo of Chester was a big orangutan. Flint recognized her as Barb.

"What! No!" Flint hurried to greet her. He opened his mouth, but Barb put her finger to his lips. She

34

projected a holographic Chester into the room.

"Good day. I have something very important to discuss with you," Hologram Chester told Flint.

The Chester-gram evaporated into the Live Corp logo and disappeared. Barb looked at Flint.

"Chester V wants to see me?" He gasped in fear. "Oh no. . . . Am I being fired because of the incident today?"

Barb simply stared at him.

Flint was freaking out. "Okay—no, no. Wait. Uhhhh . . . I—I—I just need to grab my stuff! Hold on!" He ran around manically packing items into a Live Corp orange backpack. "Dad, maybe Chester will give me another chance! Steve? Steve?" Where was his assistant? "Steve? Steve? Steve?" Flint looked around.

"Son, I don't think you should run off into the night with that monkey-person-lady-thing," Tim warned. Tim turned around to reveal that Steve was clinging to his back.

"Oh, there you are, Steve! C'mon!" Flint reached out toward Steve.

35

"Steve!" He refused to let go.

Flint pried Steve away and followed Barb out the door.

"Wish me luck," he called over his shoulder to his dad.

Tim watched from the window as Flint climbed into Barb's Live Car. He gave Flint a little wave and a half smile. Barb turned and flashed Tim a sinister smile as the hover-car flew away.

Flint, Steve, and Barb stood at the base of the Live Corp elevator. Flint bounced on his toes, uncertain what to expect. When the elevator door opened, they all stepped inside.

"Monkey . . . ," Steve said, breaking the uncomfortable silence.

"Excuse me! I'm an ape," Barb replied.

The elevator stopped and the door opened.

"Follow me." Barb stepped out onto a glass floor.

All of Live Corp could be seen through the floor. In the middle of the room, an egg-shaped orb turned to reveal Chester's private workspace. Chester rose from his chair.

"Ah, young Lockwood," he greeted.

Flint was flustered in the great inventor's presence. "Chester V, sir. I can explain everythi—" Thrusting out his hand, Flint went to shake, but like in Swallow Falls, his fingers passed through Chester. Flint lowered his hand and sighed, "I thought I was meeting the real Chester V."

"You are." The first Chester disappeared. Another took his place.

"Not me," Chester number two said. He pointed across the office. "Him."

This Chester also vaporized as Flint turned around.

"Yes, it's me," real Chester said. "Sorry about that." He stepped forward, explaining, "My holograms and I were having a brainstorming session."

Flint poked this Chester. He was real.

"Ah!" Flint said, relieved. "Mr. V, I have somthing important to say to you. Please don't fire me."

CHAPTER 6

"I'm so excited to be here and to get this opportunity to show you my inventions," Flint told Chester V. "May I present . . . the Forkenknifenspooninator! The latest in hands-free dining technology—" Before Chester could respond, Flint strapped a dangerous-looking machine to his neck. It had robot arms holding a napkin, knife, fork, and spoon.

"Hold on, hold on," Chester interrupted. "That's not why I brought you here tonight."

Reaching past Flint, Chester turned on a giant hologram TV screen. "We've received some troubling transmissions from the cleanup crew on Swallow Falls."

On the screen Flint saw a Sentinel of Safety wearing a name tag which read PETER in a bunker. He was screaming into a web cam. "There's only two of us left! We need help!" Something large jumped on top of the roof. The bunker shook violently. "Aaaaaah!" Peter screamed like a baby as giant French-fry legs punched through the top of the shelter. The roof was ripped off.

Stan, another sentinel, backed away as an enormous cheeseburger creature descended over him.

The video ended with Stan's echoing screams.

Flint and Steve stared at the screen. Both their mouths hung open.

"What is that thing?" Flint asked.

"Cheesy!" Steve said.

Chester nodded at Steve. "It appears to be a living cheeseburger. A double bacon cheeseburger with French-fry legs and sesame-seed eyes."

Flint took a second to process the information. "Living food? Oh no. This could only mean one thing—the FDLSMDFR survived the explosion and it's still operating." The Forkenknifenspooninator gave Flint a sip of water.

"It gets worse, Flint," Chester warned.

Flint spit out the water.

"This is what worries me most." Chester fast-forwarded to some grainy footage of a cheespider standing at the edge of a lagoon. It approached the water's edge, dipped its French-fry toe in, and scurried back.

"They're trying to learn to swim," Chester said. "When they succeed, they will destroy monuments all up and down the Eastern seaboard including Lady Liberty herself! Lady Liberty."

Flint put his hands up to his mouth, blocking the Forkenknifenspooninator.

Chester pointed to the orangutan. "Barb worked out an algorithm—thank you, Barb—and, unless we intervene, these soaking wet, man-eating creatures are going to reach Plymouth Rock in seventy-two hours. We have a ticking clock, young Lockwood."

"That thing that I thought could never happen again is happening. Again." Flint had a sudden headache.

"I fear for humanity," Chester told him.

"There has to be something we can do," Flint said.

"Well, my Thinkquanauts have invented this." Chester held out an orange device similar to a flash drive. "They call it the BSUSB."

Flint considered the gadget. "A Bifurcating Systematic Universal Stop Button!"

40

Chester smiled. "Precisely."

Flint shivered with pride as Chester held the device.

"It would destroy the machine and everything it created! But we cannot find the FLDSMDFR. We've searched everywhere . . . and failed."

Flint volunteered. "Chester, I can find it!"

Barb said, "I'll assemble a team of my fellow Thinkquanauts!"

Flint shook his head. "No! Thank you. I can do this on my own."

"Yes, alone. What a good idea. I admire your courage," Chester said. "If you succeed, I will make you . . . a Thinkquanaut!"

Flint gave a little squeal of excitement. Maybe his dream would come true after all! He grabbed the BSUSB from Chester and took off for the elevator. "I won't let you down!"

Flint packed in a rush and hurried out of his apartment.

He stopped at Sam's place.

41

She opened the door in her pajamas, with a mud mask smeared on her face.

"Flint? Is everything okay?" Sam asked.

"Sam, big news!" Flint took a big breath and blurted, "I'm going back to Swallow Falls to destroy the FLDSMDFR, which is creating deadly food monsters that are trying to learn to swim so they can attack Lady Liberty!"

She stared in shocked silence.

"Sam?" Flint moved his face in closer to hers.

"Wait, you're doing this alone?" she asked, slowly putting the pieces together.

"Well, yeah. But please don't tell Dad. If he finds out I'm going back to Swallow Falls, he's going to want to come too."

Across the hall, Tim overheard Flint. He opened one eye.

"Well, I'm coming!" Sam declared. She went to pack her own orange pack.

Flint stood in the hallway. "What?! No, Sam! It's going to be deadly dangerous with a good chance of death!"

The door opened again. Sam was fully dressed and ready to go.

"And that's why we'll need help," she declared.

Looking utterly unhappy, Policeman Earl was preparing a fancy latte drink for a snooty customer. His uniform was covered by an apron and a paper hat. "Triple decaf mochaccino-boba-latte with skim soy and nutmeg sprinkle?" He handed the drink to the customer.

"I'd like to order something strong!" Flint said, entering the shop.

"Wait your turn, fancy-pants—" Earl then realized who was speaking. "Flint Lockwood and Sam Sparks!" He leapt over the counter to hug them. "I missed you Flint! And Steve, too!"

"Juicy!" Steve said.

"Earl, we need your help," Flint said.

Sam explained, "Swallow Falls is overrun with deadly food monsters."

"Hey, where's my coffee!?" a customer complained.

"Coffee?! I'm not a barista, I'm a polista!" Earl tore off his apron and straightened his badge. "Let's ride!"

Cal stepped out from behind the counter wearing a chef's hat. "Can I come too, Dad?"

"Son, you are my precious little angel, but I can't let you come with me. Not until you get your first chest hair," Earl replied.

"I have chest hair!" Cal pulled down his jacket revealing a curl.

"It's just like mine," Earl beamed with pride, but then looked a little closer. "Wait a minute."

Earl wiped Cal's chest with his finger and ate the smudge. "That's not a chest hair! That's cupcake frosting. Tell your mom that I'm getting our home back." Earl hugged Cal and did a backflip out of the shop.

Manny was outside in a field, garbed in a doctor's uniform. A nurse handed him the tools he needed as he called for them.

"Sponge . . . forceps . . . swab . . ." Suddenly he

spotted Sam in the reflection of a mirror.

"Manny, we need your help," she said.

Manny looked up from his patient. He was help-ing a cow give birth. The baby calf was halfway out.

"I can drop everything." He held out a hand to the nurse. "Camera."

The nurse handed him his professional camera bag and he followed Sam out.

Brent was standing on a street corner, wearing a new yellow rubber chicken suit. He was dancing while spinning an arrow-shaped sign that read: CHICK-N-SUSHI.

The gang drove by him at first, then backed up.

"Yo! Chicken Brent!" Flint called out.

"In the flesh!" Brent replied.

Sam shouted to him, "Swallow Falls is in trouble! Will you help us? Please? Flint needs you!"

"You bet I will! I just need someone to cover my shift." He looked around for help, then wedged his sign into a branch of a nearby tree. "Thanks, tree!"

Brent squeezed his big body into the already tightly packed car, poking his head out of the sunroof as the gang drove away.

At the wharf Flint faced his friends. He stood beside his Grocery Deliverator. "Okay, gang, we'll be traveling to the island using my Grocery Deliverator!"

He plugged it in and a terrifying electric vortex appeared.

Flint stepped aside. "Alright, who wants to go first?"

The group exchanged uneasy looks.

"Hungry!" Steve was about to eat a banana sandwich.

"Yes, Steve! Hungry for adventure!" Flint scooped him up. "See you on the island, my brave lab partner! See you soon, Steve!"

"Afraid . . . ," Steve said as Flint pitched him into the vortex.

"It worked! Who's next?" Flint was ready for the next volunteer.

Just then, Steve was ejected from the Deliverator. His hair stood on end and he stumbled around in a daze. The sandwich was missing.

"STEEEEEEEEEEVE . . . !" He stumbled forward.

"Hmm, that's weird. I'm not sure what happened." Flint considered the problem.

Brent was feeling brave and ready to roll. He rushed toward the teleporter. "My turn! My turn! I'm next!"

Just at that moment a boat pulled up to the dock. The cabin door burst open.

"Ahoy there, skipper ma' boy!" Tim called out.

"Dad! No! How did you know we were here?" Flint asked.

"I could see you from the apartment." Tim pointed to the extension cord leading up to the balcony of the apartment they shared, which was only a few feet away.

"Dad, the island is going to be very dangerous." Flint tried to convince him it was a bad idea. "No." Flint was working on a list of reasons when Sam walked past him and climbed onto Tim's boat.

47

"Flint, let him help," she said.

"The man does have a boat," Earl pointed out.

"Which is twice as many boats as we have," Brent added.

"*Vamanos, muchachos!*" Manny said.

They all got onto the boat except Flint.

"Fine. But we'll get there faster if we use the Grocery Deliverator—" As he said it, Steve jumped onto Flint's back, squealing in horror.

"Steeeeeeeeeeeve!"

Flint gave up. "Okay. We'll take the boat."

"Shovin' off!" Tim maneuvered them out of the harbor, toward home.

Meanwhile, Barb was sitting in her car on the docks. She frowned as she watched them go.

48

CHAPTER 7

Tim's boat pitched and rolled across the rough ocean. Thick fog made it hard to see what was ahead.

"We'll be there in two flaps of a sardine's fluke!" Tim announced as he navigated the sea.

In the main cabin Flint and his friends rocked back and forth.

"Thanks, Dad!" Flint made notes on his computer as he explained his plan to find the FLDSMDFR. "Okay, when we land at Swallow Falls, we have to get to my lab, boot up my old computer, and use it to pinpoint the FLDSMDFR's location."

"Sounds easy," Sam said.

"Yeah, so long as we don't end up fast food for that supersized cheespider!" Flint hit a button on his computer, opening the image of the spider he'd seen in Chester V's office.

"That's why *I'm* here, Flint Lockwood," Earl said. "I'll keep us safe."

Flint noticed Brent was still wearing the rubber chicken suit. "Uh . . . Brent. Don't you want to change out of that chicken suit?"

"Well, I didn't bring any clothes. So it's either this or I put on the diaper," Brent replied.

It was unanimous. Everyone shouted at the same time, "Chicken suit it is!"

Just then Tim announced their arrival. "Land ho! Land ho!"

The gang all turned to look.

Flint was certain they could conquer the cheespider. "If we all work together, this should be a—"

"Piece of cake!" Manny interrupted, pointing toward the island.

The fog parted and Flint saw a gigantic piece of cake floating in the water. Flint gasped and rushed out onto the deck. "We're—"

"Toast!" Sam stared at the sea.

"French toast!" Earl raised his hand over his eyes to see as far as he could.

All around them, giant pieces of toast floated on the water's surface.

"This is totally—" Flint began.

"Bananas!" Steve finished.

A bunch of gigantic bananas was straight ahead of the boat.

Their beloved Sardine Falls cannery was shrouded in fog, but they could all see it had a big hole in its middle.

Tim expertly steered through the debris to the boat dock. The island vegetation had grown into a dark and foreboding jungle.

"Home!" Steve jumped off the boat and ran up the dock. He swung himself up to stand on the CHEWANDSWALLOW sign.

"No! Steve! Wait!" Flint went after Steve, but when he stepped on the rotting dock, he nearly fell through a loose board. "Whoa! Be careful!" he told the others.

Sam and the rest moved slowly down the gang-plank behind him. "Manny! Are you getting this?"

"I certainly am." Manny's camera panned the area.

51

Sam used her Doppler to find a pathway through the jungle. "This is amazing. Look. The climate must have shifted dramatically to allow this much vegetation to grow!"

Flint stepped closer to Sam as an ominous growl echoed around them. Eyes glowed from the shadows. A flock of ratbirds burst from the foliage.

"Aaah! Ratbird!" Sam and Flint shouted at the same time.

One of the ratbirds hovered near Flint's face. It squawked and flew away. Tim came off the boat, carrying a harpoon gun, a duffle bag and—a smile. "Okay then. All ashore who's going ashore!"

"Dad." Flint blocked his way. "Why don't you stay and guard the boat?"

"Guard the boat?" Tim looked at Flint as if he was crazy.

The gang agreed with Flint. Tim was outnumbered. They put on their orange Live Corp backpacks for the journey. He was stuck staying behind.

"Bye, Dad! Be back by suppertime!" Flint said before walking away.

"Sure. Fine . . ." Tim lowered his weapon and sighed.

A few feet into the bushes, Earl became the leader. He peeked through some heavy food growth.

"Whoa . . . look what's happened to our town," Flint said.

Earl pointed. "Look, there's my angel son Cal's old preschool."

Manny pointed. "There's my old van."

Brent pointed. "Look, there's that old thing I've never seen before!"

A Live Corp bunker was ahead. It was completely torn up and covered in a cheese web.

Flint considered the find. "That's where the Thinkquanauts were attacked by a cheespider."

"Let's get out of here!" Brent shouted.

Sam disagreed. "No, wait . . . what if there's a survivor in there?"

"I'll check it out," Earl said. Earl flipped a few times then rolled closer to the bunker. "Hello? Anybody in here?"

The gang cautiously followed the policeman inside the empty bunker.

Suddenly a box fell off a shelf. They all jumped back.

"Hah!" Earl bravely moved toward the box. The rest of the gang awkwardly held out pretend finger guns to cover him.

Earl carefully flipped the lid, revealing a giant strawberry.

"Wow," Flint said.

"That is the biggest strawberry I've ever seen in my life," Sam noted.

Flint bent down and picked it up.

"Is it heavy?" Brent asked, leaning in.

"Yeah. But other than that, it looks like a perfectly normal, fresh, delicious strawberry." Flint turned the strawberry over in his hand and was suddenly face-to-face with a blinking creature. "Aaaaaah!" Flint screamed.

"Aaaaaah!" the strawberry screamed.

"Aaaaaah!" everybody screamed.

Flint dropped the berry and jumped into Earl's arms.

"N-woo," the strawberry said.

"It's moving!" Brent pointed in fear.

The strawberry chased the gang from the bunker.

"Phew! That was a close one." Flint breathed easy once they were a safe distance away.

"You got a little someone stuck to your pants!" Sam said, staring down toward Flint's feet.

The little strawberry was hugging Flint's leg and cooing, "N-woo!"

"Aaaagh! Get it off! Get if off! Sam! Sam!" Flint kicked his legs madly. The strawberry giggled, enjoying the ride.

"Wait! Wait! Stop!" Sam picked up the berry and cradled it in her hands.

"Sam! Don't touch it! Put it down! Put it down!" Flint was freaking out.

"Look at him!" Sam calmed Flint. She turned the little guy around. He was adorable.

Flint stepped back as little hands reached out for a hug. *"Aaaaaaaaahhhhhhh!"*

Sam laughed at Flint. "Seriously? Aw, I think I'll name him Barry."

Flint refused to come any closer. "Sam, could

you please put Barry down?"

"N-woo, N-woo!" Barry cooed.

No time to mess around with live strawberries. Flint said, "We have to get to the FLDSMDFR so we can shut it down with this utterly irreplaceable BSUSB." He held up the BSUSB. Barry grabbed it and jumped free. "Hey! That is *not* for you!"

Barry ran away.

Flint chased him. "I need that! *Please!* That BSUSB is really important!"

Barry stopped and turned around. He looked up at Flint with adoration. "N-woo?"

"N-woo! Yes!" Flint inched slowly closer to him.

"Hi, N-woo." Flint bent down to Barry's level. "Hey, you want to hand it to me buddy? I beg you. Pleeease."

"N-woo," Barry said.

"N-woo, N-woo, yes! Yes. There ya go . . ." Flint reached out his hand.

Barry stared for a beat, then swallowed the device.

"Noooooooo!" Flint shouted.

Barry hurried off into the jungle.

Flint shot Brent a look.

With no other option, the gang chased Barry through the jungle. He ducked into the roofless restaurant. And so did they.

CHAPTER 8

Barry left through the back of restaurant, and the gang continued to chase him.

"Don't let him get away!" Flint said.

Barry skipped through some water. It slowed him down long enough for Flint to catch up. "Gotcha!"

"N-woo?" Barry asked.

"Ah! Here, you take it! You take it!" Flint passed Barry to Sam. "You're going to have to carry him until he passes the BSUSB."

Sam grimaced. "And by pass, you mean . . ." She wrinkled her nose as if she smelled something bad.

"Yes. Look, we better get a move on before we run into any more of these creatures."

As Sam and Flint talked, the rest of the gang noticed something straight ahead. They gasped. Sardine Circle, the center of town, was now a waterhole for a ton of living food creatures! Wildebeets bathed. Bananostriches flocked. Hippotatomuses lounged. The buildings of the town loomed large all around them.

"It's so beautiful!" Sam gushed. The island was now like a wild nature park.

"Wow," Flint said. "I can't believe the FLDSMDFR created all of this." He looked around, suddenly realizing the strawberry was missing. "Where's Barry?"

Flint and Sam stared at each other.

"Wheeeeeeeeeeee!" Barry was happily floating down the river.

"Uh-oh," Earl said. "Here we go again."

The gang found a police car. Earl paddled it like a raft across the watering hole in pursuit of Barry.

"Just a little bit closer," Flint told Earl.

"N-woooooo!" Barry giggled.

"Look at the mangos!" Sam said as the car-boat coasted through a flock of mango-birds.

"You mean flamingos," Flint corrected her.

"Fla*mangos*!" Sam told him.

"There's a bunch of shrimp!" Brent pointed out a group of shrieking crustaceans that were jumping across the canopy of the jungle.

"They look like chimpanzees," Manny said.

"Shrimpanzees!" Brent and Manny gave them a new name.

They passed under city hall, closing in on the little strawberry.

Flint pleaded to Barry. "Barry! C'mon, Chester gave me that BSUSB! It's really important!"

Suddenly a shrimpanzee jumped down onto the car and grabbed Steve's thought translator.

"Shrimpanzee!" The creature was now able to speak.

Steve yanked it off the creature and put it back on himself. "Steve!"

The shrimpanzee scowled and snagged it back. "Shrimpanzee!"

"Steve!"

"Shrimpanzee!"

Steve grabbed the translator for the last time before shoving the shrimpanzee into the river. "Shove . . . Steve!"

The translator battle over, Flint noticed something

in the car. "There's a leek in the boat! Aaah!"

Flint didn't mean the boat had a "leak" and was filling with water. He meant a "leek," as in the vegetable. A leek was sitting behind the steering wheel. It turned to Flint, then screamed back at him. The boat began to pick up speed.

"Oh no!" Sam grabbed Flint's arm.

"Hold on, everyone," Earl warned the crew. "This ain't gonna be no picnic!"

They passed through a spot where the river narrowed and spilled out into a whirlpool.

Even as they spun around, Flint was still trying to get Barry. "Stop! Get back here! Keep it steady, Earl! I've almost got him!"

He was so close, when a watermelophant rose out of the water with Barry perched on its back.

"Watermelophants!" Sam was awed.

Another watermelophant clumped into the river, creating a big wave and sending the car over a waterfall.

"Aaaaaah!" The gang shouted in one big voice.

"Barry! Grab my hand!! Barry!" Flint called out to the strawberry.

The car landed with a splash and floated through the rapids.

Finally Barry spun into a calm eddy.

"Freeze, berryman!" the policeman said. "You have the right to remain tasty." Earl scooped him up with a spoon, handing him off to Sam.

"Thanks, Earl." Flint was grateful.

Sam looked at Flint in amazement. "I can't believe your machine reprogrammed itself to create this entire ecosystem of living food. How is that even possible?"

"I have no idea," Flint replied.

"It's incredible," Sam said. "The world should know about this."

Meanwhile, a drone hidden in a tree was filming everything that was happening so Chester V could watch from his office at Live Corp. Chester and Barb were watching the boat from a computer screen in Chester's office.

"'The world should know about this,'" Barb repeated. "So much for keeping this a secret."

"We can't let these friends tell the world anything,

or distract Flint from his mission," Chester said. "What we need to do is go there and turn Flint against his friends."

Chester's holograms all started cheering at once.

"Brilliant idea!"

"Way to go, Chester!"

"Yes!"

"Yes!"

"Thank you, all," Chester said modestly. He turned to Barb. "Barb, you take care of that weather girl."

Barb wasn't happy. "But, sir, I'm a scientist!" she protested.

Chester smiled. "That's why I need you. I need your brilliant mind to help me save Live Corp."

Barb blushed at the compliment. "Consider it done, sir!"

Chester clapped his hands. "Good monkey!" he shouted. "To the helpicopter!"

It wasn't really a power line. It was a web trap for the cheespider. The spider opened its sesame-seed eyes and looked around. As Earl parked the police car at the river's edge, the cheespider's vision focused in on their orange backpacks.

Sam stashed Barry safely in her pack. "Okay, come here. You have caused enough trouble for one day."

Brent was glad to be on solid ground. "Woo-hoo! Yeah! Hey guys, that wasn't so bad."

"Yeah," Flint agreed. "We'll be thankful we didn't run into a—"

A roar came from directly behind them.

"*Cheespider!*" Flint ran into the wild jungle without looking back.

"*Cheespider! Cheespider!*" Sam said over and over.

"Cheesy! Cheesy! Cheesy!" Steve repeated.

Earl picked up Steve as he sprinted forward. Then Earl picked up Manny and tucked him under his other arm. "Manny!"

Brent was left trailing behind. "Hey! Wait for me!"

The cheespider was spitting cheese wads as he

went. His gnashing teeth caught Brent's orange Live Corp backpack.

Brent struggled to free himself. The cheespider chomped down on the backpack, popping him out of the rubber chicken suit. Launched into the air wearing only his diaper, Brent landed on Earl's back.

"I'm glad you're still wearing that diaper," Earl commented.

The cheespider swallowed the backpack, chicken suit and all.

"Hey guys, down this alley!" Flint thought he saw a way out of the jungle. He headed into an alley but slammed into something. Flint fell backward. "Oof."

The alley was actually a fallen billboard advertising SWALLOW FALLS ALLEYS: BUILDING QUALITY ALLEYS SINCE 2009!

"Oh no, dead end!" Sam gasped.

"Dead," Steve said sadly.

Flint tried to hide behind his Live Corp backpack. The cheespider moved closer, chomping at Flint.

Suddenly heat lamps dropped down from the sky,

65

singeing the cheespider and causing it to retreat into the jungle. The heat lamps pulled back into the bottom of a Live Corp Help-icopter.

Chester V had arrived—just in the nick of time.

CHAPTER 9

"Ghost man?!" Earl was surprised to see Chester step out of the Help-icopter.

"Greetings and Namaste," Chester V said.

"Chester V! You're here?" Flint was even more surprised than Earl to see the great inventor in Swallow Falls.

"That's right, young Lockwood!" Chester told Flint. "And by the looks of things, just in time."

"One minute later and we would have been food for that food!" Earl was grateful to have been saved.

Chester lowered his eyes at Flint. "Flint, I thought you said you were going to complete this mission *alone*?"

"Oh . . . uh," Flint said slowly. "These are my friends. They're the bravest, smartest people I know."

As he said the word "brave," Brent began to

shout, "Help! Help, help, help!" Wearing only his diaper, Brent rushed around, frantically stomping at his feet. "My shoes! They're totally covered in worms! Oooh! Aaah! Oooh! Aaah!" He suddenly calmed down. "Oh, wait, those are my toes. Never mind!"

Chester flashed a baffled look at Flint.

"Heh, heh." Flint shrugged.

"I suppose bringing them along shows initiative," Chester remarked.

Steve reached out for Chester's mustache. "Mustache!"

Chester forced the monkey back. Then said to Flint, "I should have never let you go alone in the first place. Good job!"

Barb joined the group. "Can I say something?"

Everyone but Flint reacted with shock at the talking ape.

"Apparently you can," Manny muttered.

Chester made the introduction. "This is Barb. My number two."

Barb asked Sam, "Why are you carrying a strawberry in your backpack, Miss?" She yanked Barry out of Sam's backpack by his leafy ankles.

"Stand back, everyone!" Chester warned, eyeing the strawberry suspiciously.

"Hey! Stop! You're scaring him!" Sam told Barb.

"Scaring him? Oh please, it's probably got a mouth full of fangs." Barb held Barry tighter.

Sam put her hands on her hips. "I've been carrying him and he hasn't hurt anyone."

Barb was not impressed. "I'm sorry, are you a scientist?"

"As a matter of fact, I am," Sam said.

"She's a meteorologist," Flint proudly told Barb.

"Meteorology. I love it." Barb laughed. "The science of smiling and having pretty hair while you point at a map."

"Actually it's a very important job—" Flint began, but Sam was prepared to defend herself.

She retorted to Barb, "Meteorology is a comprehensive analysis of atmospheric—"

Chester stepped between them and said, "Ladies, ladies, please. I'm sure we can all agree that one of you is a scientist," and leaned toward Barb.

Sam flashed Flint a look. She was clearly insulted.

Flint didn't know what to say, so he shrugged sympathetically.

"The key thing to remember is that we cannot trust these creatures." Chester pointed at Barry.

Barry snapped at Chester.

The inventor pulled his finger away just in time. "Ahhh! See? No matter how innocent they may appear, they are still vicious and aggressive."

"That doesn't mean we have to be," Sam said.

Chester glared at Sam for a beat, then turned away from her. "Young Lockwood, why was your lady friend carrying this rabid little strawberry in her backpack?"

"Why is the strawberry guy in the backpack?" Flint had to tell the truth. He sighed. "He ate the BSUSB."

"Not the BSUSB!" Chester's face flushed red.

"I'm on it." Barb snapped on rubber gloves and whipped out a scalpel.

"Watch out!" Earl shouted. "She's got a knife!"

Sam snatched Barry away from Barb. "Don't you dare touch a leaf on his head!" she warned the ape.

"Step away from the berry, madame," Barb said. She advanced toward Barry, his strawberry eyes widening in fear. Suddenly, *splat!* A small heap of strawberry jelly hit the ground with the BSUSB floating inside.

"N-woo?" Barry was embarrassed.

Earl clapped his hands. "That orange hairy lady scared the jelly out of him!"

Barry leaped away, escaping into the jungle.

Flint picked up the BSUSB. The function light was glowing solid red. "Oh no. It's jammed!"

"Lick, lick, lick." Steve licked the jelly out of it.

The light turned green.

"Oh. Thanks, Steve," Flint said.

Chester pulled Flint away from the others. "Young Lockwood, the world could have been destroyed because of the actions of one sinister strawberry. We cannot allow any more mistakes like this. It won't be long before those malicious melons, pernicious pickles, and belligerent burgers learn to swim and make their way to the mainland. What is your plan?"

Flint actually did have a plan. He explained,

"Um, I need to get back to my lab so I can make contact with my FLDSMDFR."

"Brilliant!" Chester was pleased. "Let's take my Help-icopter."

Eager to get out of there, they all faced the Help-i-copter just as it sunk into the ground. It turned out the soil wasn't actually soil—it was oatmeal.

"Better plan: We'll go on foot," Chester said.

Earl performed a fancy action flip to the front of the group. "Alright. I'll lead the way."

"No, *we'll* lead the way," Sentinel of Safety Louise said as three Sentinels of Safety flipped to a spot in front of him.

Chester pushed Earl aside, saying, "I believe my Sentinels of Safety are better equipped to lead us in their Robo-Suits."

As they headed into the jungle, Barry peeked out of the bushes and watched them go. "N-woo?" he asked.

On the way to Flint's lab, Brent borrowed some real clothes from Flint. He picked a T-shirt that said, I GOT BRAINS.

"Ooh, look!" Sam said. "Sardine Crescent!"

"We're close! Sir, my lab should be straight up ahead—" Flint yelled to Chester, as a large stampede of bananostriches ran by.

OOOF!

Flint smacked his head on a low hanging mailbox, wrapped in vines.

"Ohhh, are you okay?" Sam checked the bruise.

Flint shook it off. The mailbox said LOCKWOOD on the side. Flint moved the vines aside for a better look at the situation. His home had been lifted up into a giant tree. The rooms were spread across different branches.

Steve was happy to be there no matter what the house looked like. "Home! Home! Home!" he repeated.

"Or what's left of it." Flint frowned.

"Oh my gosh, your lab!" Sam showed Flint a branch where his lab dangled from the canopy of the vines. One big wind and it would fall, smashing to smithereens.

"We can't go up there, Flint Lockwood," Earl said. "That dangly upsy-downsy lab's not to code."

"But if I'm going to find the FLDSMDFR, I've got to!" Flint studied the problem.

"We can do it," Sam said. "Those load-bearing vines will be able to support a small team."

Chester ignored Sam, telling Flint, "Excellent! Onwards and upwards!"

"Right, sir! To the lab!" Flint rushed to the porta-potty and jumped in, wiggling himself up the tube.

Chester followed Flint, but told his sentinels to stay on the ground. "Sentinels! Keep the locals safe." The sentinels surrounded Earl and Manny.

Brent saw Sam sneak into the tube. "Hey, guys, where you going? Guys?" He didn't want to be left behind. "Hey, wait for me!" Brent dove into the porta-potty but got stuck. "Uh-oh. Um, little help?"

CHAPTER 10

Flint and Chester crawled up into Flint's laboratory. Just behind them, Sam struggled to keep up with Barb.

"Seems like only yesterday I was in this porta-potty for the very first time," Sam remarked.

Flint opened the door and peered down the darkened hallway to his lab.

"Spooky!" Steve said.

"Spooky is right, Steve!" Flint said, stepping carefully onto the lab floor. The entire lab tilted and shook.

Chester followed him in. "I say, this laboratory of yours is a wonder of engineering!"

"Really? Thank you, sir!" Flint turned on the power and said, "Initiating backup power! Beep, boop, boop, boop, beep."

The lab lit up. Cords and monitors dangled into a pool of water, causing sparks and electric pulses. Flint's computer was dead, hanging lifelessly inches above the pool.

"So how are we supposed to locate the FLDSMDFR if the computer is fried?" Barb asked.

Flint tripped forward, slipping toward the electrified water.

"Flint!" Chester grabbed Flint by the seat of his underpants. They stretched out like a rubber safety line. "I say, young Lockwood, what extraordinary underpants!" With a huge tug, he yanked Flint back to safety.

"Thank you, sir! They're my Wedgie-Proof Underwear!" Flint said. "I invented them when I was six."

"I had no idea we were so alike. Except I invented mine when I was three." Chester showed Flint his own Wedgie-Proof Underwear.

Sam asked, "You guys have been wearing the same underwear since you were kids?"

"Yes!" Flint and Chester snapped their underwear at the same moment.

Barb rolled her eyes and got back to business. "Excuse me, how do you expect us to get that hard drive with all of that electrified water?"

"We dangle! Come Lockwood, give the monkey your underpants!" Chester said.

"What?" Barb was disgusted.

Chester and Flint both stretched out their undies and gave her the band to hold.

"Lay on, young Lockwood!" Chester said.

On the count of three, the two men leapt off the edge toward the electrified pool below.

Barb told Sam, "Well, at least *I* have something important to do . . ."

Sam was sick of Barb's insults. She simply looked away.

"You know," Chester told Flint as they swung through the lab, collecting equipment. "Hanging from my underpants in this space brings back so many memories. Unfortunately they were not happy ones. I, too, built my lab up high to keep the bullies out."

Flint bounced past him. "You were bullied too?"

Chester bounced off a wall. "Absolutely! People like us are always bullied."

Flint landed gently on his computer and opened it to get the hard drive.

Chester sighed. "Sometimes I wish I'd kept my bullies around so I could crush them with my success, just like you did with that man-baby."

Flint climbed up from the computer, hard drive in hand. "You mean Brent? Sure, he used to be a bully, but he's my friend now."

As Flint pushed off, Chester caught him, turning Flint around and looking at him squarely.

"Friend?" Chester shook his head. "A bully can never be your friend. I see how he treats you."

"Um. Nicely?" Flint didn't understand what Chester was talking about.

"He's manipulating you, Flint," Chester said. "Getting your guard down—and then he'll strike. You can never trust a bully. Remember the ancient Chinese proverb, '*E gun gei de shi wu ken ding you du!*'" He translated, "Stew offered by a bully is poisoned broth."

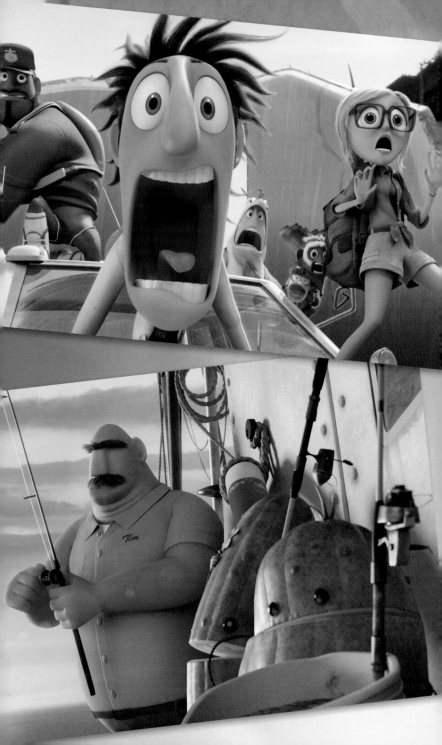

Flint was shocked. "Wow, stew," he said, considering it. "I have so much to learn."

While they were spinning and talking, Flint and Chester's underpants twisted together like a braid. They untangled, then landed near Barb and Sam.

"I think we've got everything," Flint said, showing all the equipment he'd gathered.

"Well done, Lockwood!" Chester cheered. "Well done."

CHAPTER 11

Below the lab Manny was struggling to pull Brent out of the porta-potty.

Finally Barb pushed Brent from behind. He popped right out.

Flint popped out next. "Ha-ha! We did it! That was exciting!" he declared.

Chester said, "No, Lockwood, *you* did it." He looked to the sky. "Alas, dusk is upon us. Sentinels, make camp."

The sentinels saluted and rushed away.

Chester leaned in to Flint. "Finish the tracking device, and come first light . . ."

Flint finished the thought. ". . . we'll find my FLDSMDFR!"

Chester winked and left with the sentinels.

Flint looked up at the setting sun and said, "This

job is turning out to be more dangerous than I thought. Who would have thought my FLDSMDFR would have caused so much trouble? I hope Dad's doing okay back on the boat."

Tim wasn't at the boat. He had taken his harpoon and started out through the jungle. "'I'll be back before supper.' Hmph. What a bucket of bologna! Just leave me on the boat without any food? Well, I know a place where I can get something to eat."

He climbed a ridge overlooking the tackle shop. "There she is. Home sweet home."

Tim entered the shop and flipped the sign from CLOSED to OPEN. The shelves were bare, and empty sardine cans littered the floor.

"What? There's no sardines? Gotta be looters." He powered up the generator. The banks of fluorescent lights clicked on. He knelt down behind the counter and spun the dial on a safe. Behind the steel door, Tim had stashed a stack of vintage Baby Brent brand sardine cans. "Ah. Vintage Baby Brent." He opened a can and savored the aroma. As Tim lifted a sardine to his mouth, the doorbell rang. He was so surprised, he toppled backward to the floor.

"Ow!"

Peeking over the countertop, Tim saw a group of pickles carrying fishing rods like spears. The pickles scavenged through the empty sardine cans, looking for any unopened ones.

Tim ducked back behind the counter, grabbing his harpoon gun. The loose fitting harpoon shot out from the gun. Tim leaned forward to grab the harpoon, but a pickle got there first. Tim backed into the corner, trying to hide. The pickle noticed him and rushed at him with the pointy end of the harpoon.

"Gurble! Gurb-gurb-gurb-burb!" the pickle said.

"No! No!" Tim flinched, but the pickle unexpectedly skewered a sardine from Tim's can. The pickle put the sardine in its mouth, chewing.

"Uh-huh." Tim ate a sardine too. "Yeah. I like 'em, too. I do. I love 'em."

The pickle tried to take the can from Tim. They were playing tug-of-war.

"Mine! No! Mine!"

"Garble-garble!" the pickle argued.

The rest of the pickles came around the corner. They began to fight with one another for the last of the sardines.

"Hey, hey, hey! Easy guys! Come on, you could lose an eye!" Tim tried to break it up, but the pickles turned on Tim, raising their fishing rods as weapons.

One of the pickles picked up the empty sardine can and pointed at it.

"I tell you what," Tim told them. "You want more sardines? I can get ya more sardines!"

As the Sentinels of Safety kept watch, Flint and his friends were hard at work inside Flint's old house.

Manny had just finished preparing dinner, when outside something roared in the jungle.

"Sounds like midnight snacks," Manny said.

"Mmmm." Brent licked his lips. "Dr. Manny! This is delicious!"

Flint rushed through the room, carrying the things he needed for his newest invention.

"Hey, guys. Smells good." He took a big sniff.

"Flint! Wanna try some of this special stew? I saved you a bowl. It's killer!" Brent held out a spoon.

"Killer stew?" Flint was suddenly very nervous. In his head, he heard the words to Chester's Chinese proverb. *E gun gei de shi wu ken ding you du!*

Flint knocked the bowl out of Brent's hand. "No!"

The gang looked stunned at the stew splattered across the floor.

Flint stuttered, "Th-th-thank you, Brent," then rushed from the room.

"Ever since ghost man showed up, Flint Lockwood's been acting—" Earl searched for the right word.

Steve looked at his own meal and said, "Jerky!"

"Yeah, really jerky," Brent agreed.

"He rejected my stew. No one has ever rejected my stew." Manny stared down at the mess Flint caused.

"I'm going to go talk to him." Sam went down the hallway and caught up with Flint near the fuse box. "Flint, wait up!"

"Yeah, Sam?" He turned.

"Is something wrong?" she asked.

"Yeah, we blew a fuse," he told her.

"Not that," she said. "You're acting . . . super weird."

"I've always acted super weird." Flint looked at her sideways.

"Yeah, that's true. But not like this! You karate-chopped Manny's stew out of Brent's hand. You hurt their feelings," Sam explained.

"Sam, you wouldn't understand. *E gun gei de shi wu ken ding you du!*" He repeated the proverb.

"I do understand, but you're forgetting that . . ." She replied in perfect Chinese, *"Un bah be-in chuhng pung yo yoong youan shuh pung yo."*

"Huh?" Flint couldn't believe it. She spoke Chinese!

Sam told him the rest of the saying. "'A bully turned friend, will be friend to the end.' Listen, Brent came here to help you. We *all* did." She spit on the fuse, screwed it in, and flipped a switch. The lights went on in Flint's room.

"And you're acting like we're just in your way! Remember?" Sam handed him the Sparkswood drawing. "We *work* together." She gave him one last, long look, then walked away.

85

Barb was eavesdropping. Chester too. They didn't like what they heard.

Tim anchored his boat.

"Okay, guys, we're here!" One of the pickles was wearing Tim's fishing hat. "Hey! That is *not* for you." He snagged the hat from the pickle and hung it back on a hook. "Alright, let's get to it!"

Tim grabbed a fishing rod from the wall and walked quickly from the cabin to the deck. The pickles waddled out behind him.

Tim held up his fishing rod. He grunted in a cave-man voice, "Okay. You got this, right?"

"Gurgle?" The pickles imitated his growl.

Tim tossed them lures. "Okay then—you wanna put one of these on there like this." He attached a lure to his rod.

The pickles imitated him, doing the same. Except one pickle. He ate the lure.

"No, no, don't eat that! That's bad! You'll hurt yourself," Tim warned.

A bigger pickle slapped his brother.

"Hey, easy! Stop picking on your brother, will ya? How would you like it if he was shoving you?" Parenting pickles was hard work.

The pickle slapped his brother again.

Tim gave up. "Okay, now watch. Are you watching?" He raised his pole toward the water. "One, and a two, and three! Catch the big one!" He cast the line.

"Oooh!" The pickles looked over the edge of the boat with curiosity.

Tim reeled the line back in and showed the pickles that he'd caught a sardine. "Yeah, good huh? It's called fishin'!" The pickles were in awe.

The pickles used their fishing rods properly and cast out their lines.

A little pickle tooted the boat horn.

Tim smiled. "I tell ya, if only Flint liked fishin' as much as you guys." He shook his head and muttered, "Why am I talking to a pickle?"

CHAPTER 12

The Sentinels of Safety were doing a morning check of the camp when Sam decided to follow them. Suddenly sensors on the sentinels' chest plates went off.

"Dangerous food creature detected," one sentinel announced. "We'll find and destroy it."

"Safe! Safe! Safe!" the other sentinels chanted as they all sped away.

Sam turned her head to watch them go, and heard giggling. She touched her hair and discovered Barry stuck to the back of her head.

"Babadoo!" Barry said happily.

"Barry! You can't be here!" Sam said.

Sam was trying to figure out what to do with Barry when Flint came out of his bedroom. "Ready, gang!"

They all gathered in the front yard.

Sam didn't want Flint to see Barry, so she tossed him to Manny, who quickly slipped him into Sam's backpack. Flint was wearing his Flint Lockwood Food Jungle Topographical Pointing Machine (FLFJTPM for short) on his head. Chester, Barb, and the sentinels followed close behind. Finally they were ready to go.

Flint activated the FLFJTPM, and its laser shot through a bush at the edge of the yard.

"Chester. You, me, and Barb should take the lead. Sentinels, cover us and keep us safe." As Flint said it, the sentinels saluted him.

"Brilliant!" Chester said. "Let's go."

Flint began to walk away without ever mentioning his friends.

Earl called out, "What about us?"

"Oh, right." Flint looked as though he'd forgotten all about them. "Guys! Your job is to stay safe, and bring up the rear."

"I'm about to bring my foot up his rear!" Earl muttered.

Flint walked off with his Live Corp pals. His friends

89

followed with clumping, angry footsteps.

Sam took Barry out and set him on the ground out of sight of the others.

"Now you get. Go on, get!" She set him free. For a minute Sam thought she was going to cry, but she stopped herself in the nick of time.

Barry started toward the bushes, but he stopped before disappearing. He looked at Sam one more time with a sad puppy dog expression.

"Babbady!" Barry said.

"Get out of here, Barry! That's right, go!" Sam commanded.

Finally Barry went off into the jungle.

"Bye," Sam whispered softly, and then she hurried to catch the others.

Swallow Falls had become home to all kinds of food animals.

A mosquitoast landed on a buttoad sitting atop a pancake pad.

"Butter," croaked the buttoad.

"Parkay," the mosquitoast said as she sucked out the butter, flattening the toad.

Flint moved around bacon trees to the other side of the maple syrup bog.

"Almost there. The FLDSMDFR should be just across this syrup bog." Flint swatted at a mosquitoast that was buzzing near his head.

"This is syrup? Syrup is my favorite!" Brent slapped a mosquitoast. Its little toast wings shook off the slap and the bug flew off. "Darn mosquitoasts."

Sam was annoyed. She couldn't keep silent any longer. "Wait, Flint. What if we're making a big mistake?"

"Mistake?" Flint turned to look at her.

"About shutting off the FLDSMDFR. Some of these creatures . . . they might actually be nice!" she said.

"Nonsense." Chester sneered at her. "Flint, you saw the video where my Thinkquanauts were attacked."

"He's right, Sam. I mean, we were almost eaten by a cheespider." Flint kept on the path.

Sam stepped up next to him. "I know, but except

for that one incident, the rest of the food's been friendly."

"It is true," Manny said. "The dessert creatures are especially sweet."

Flint replied, "Okay . . . maybe . . . erf—"

Barb smacked Flint hard in the face. "Mosquitoast. It was gonna bite you," she said as if she'd saved him. Flint wasn't so sure.

"See?" Chester pointed at more bothersome bugs. "Even the tiniest creatures are attacking us!" The older inventor flicked Flint on the back of the head.

"The only reason they're biting is because of the drop in barometric pressure. Bugs do that before a storm, and by the look of those nimbostratus clouds, I'd say we're in for a downpour." Sam pointed to the sky. It was full of dark clouds.

Chester told Sam, "Ms. Sparks, we are not talking about *the weather*, we are talking about food here. Dangerous food that does not have human emotion. Food that is not friendly. Food that cannot love!"

Flint was considering Chester's words when Sam said, "Flint, we should be *studying* the food animals, not destroying them. What if he's wrong?"

Chester leaned in and whispered to Flint. "The choice is yours, son. Live up to your full potential, or walk away and let the food monsters destroy Lady Liberty."

Flint felt trapped. He tried to reason with Sam.

"Sam, finding that FLDSMDFR and saving the world . . . that's what matters."

"Really? *Our* opinion doesn't matter?" Sam shouted.

"Of course it does!" Flint answered nervously. "Yes! Yes, it matters . . . just . . . not right now."

"Wellll . . ."

Sam's face grew bright red.

Brent said, "Uh-oh!"

"Wrong answer," Earl told Flint.

Sam stomped her foot. "Need I remind you that *my* science saved a whole town from a hurricane last month?"

"Sure you saved a town, but, I'm saving the world," Flint told Sam.

"Excellent. Let's go," Chester parted some bushes to make a path.

Sam wasn't done. She had more to say. "Flint, you helped me believe in myself. That I was a good scientist. You said that we work well together. Have you forgotten about Sparkswood?"

"No! No, of course not!" Flint pulled out the drawing. "But Sam, we have to stay focused. Finding that FLDSMDFR and saving the world—that's what matters." He held up the drawing. "This is just a piece of paper."

"Yeah, well, so is this, young Lockwood." She smacked the orange vest sticky note from the drawing on his Live Corp orange vest. "I'll just see you back on the boat."

She let the sticky note fall into the syrup and stomped away.

Flint went after her. "Wait, Sam. Wait, please. No, no, Sam come back. Come back, Sam! No, no, Sam! Sam! Sam!"

Sam struggled through the thick, sticky syrup.

"Saaaaaaaaaammm!" Flint shouted her name. She didn't stop.

"Earl, would you talk to her?" Flint asked.

"You bet I will," Earl said. "Hey, Sam! Wait for me!"

Manny followed Earl. Steve and Brent left too.

"What just happened?" Flint was alone with Chester and Barb. He picked up the syrupy Sparkswood drawing.

"Oh." Flint watched his friends leave.

"Sentinels! Keep them safe." Chester pointed and the sentinels rushed after Sam and the others.

Flint was watching his friends make their way through the syrup. Chester put his arm around him and guided him forward.

Then, just as Sam predicted, it started to rain.

95

CHAPTER 13

Sam, Earl, Brent, and Manny hiked through the rainy jungle.

Sam grew more and more angry with each step she took. "I told them a storm was coming, but did they listen? Nooo. Because they don't think meteorology is important enough to listen to."

"It is disheartening," Manny agreed.

"Infuriating is what it is! I just don't trust that Chester," Sam said.

Earl plucked an umbrella shaped plant to cover them. "My chest hair doesn't trust Chester."

"I can't believe Flint is still listening to that guy!" Sam exclaimed with a huff.

"It appears he is being manipulated for some nefarious purpose," Manny noted.

"Of course he is!" Sam said.

Suddenly the gang stopped in their tracks.

"Sam! Freeze!" Earl whisper-yelled.

"What?" Sam asked.

"Stay calm and walk toward me slowly," Earl instructed.

"Ve-ry slow-ly," Brent said.

As Sam turned toward them, a cheespider rose up behind her.

"Ugh, come on—now *you're* acting weird. I'm in no mood for this." She put her hands on her hips and huffed.

The cheespider grunted, spraying her with condiments.

"Aaaah!" Sam shrieked.

The cheespider roared at her.

Earl rushed to her defense. "Stop right there, cheese monster! Nobody eats my friends on my watch."

"No, Earl, wait!" Sam put her hand on Earl's shoulder, stopping him. "Chester's been lying to us about these creatures, and I am going to prove it."

She walked toward the cheespider while the gang watched in horror.

97

"Sam, don't do it!" Earl warned. "It's food-icide!"

Sam inched closer to the cheespider, extending her hand. "Nice cheespider."

Steve bounced around nervously. "Danger! Danger! Danger!"

The cheespider opened its mouth to bite Sam, but licked her instead. When she pulled away, her palm was covered in mustard.

"Ugh," Sam said.

"Yellow!" Steve noted.

"Dude! You got special-sauced!" Brent told Sam.

"It's okay, guys!" Sam said, petting the spider. "See? She's not mean. She's just a little beefy."

The cheespider panted like a friendly dog. Brent touched her and her eyes popped open. She rolled onto her side and used her French-fry leg to point at her belly.

"Whoa! What's it doing?" Brent backed away.

"I think she wants you to scratch her buns." Sam giggled.

"Awww. I like that too." Brent tickled the cheespider. "Who's a good cheespider? She's cute!" He rubbed her belly.

98

"But why did she attack us before?" Earl wondered. Sam looked around the forest. She pointed at a web, which was littered with orange Live Corp gear: shirts, mugs, hats. "Because we were dressed like *them*!" Brent's rubber chicken suit was stuck in the trees. The suit had the Live Corp backpack still attached to it.

"She doesn't like backpacks?" Brent asked.

Manny groaned. "No. It appears she doesn't like Live Corp! The food creatures know something we do not. And we need to find out what it is."

Manny opened his camera's screen. The Live Corp logo appeared for a moment. Manny hit a button on the screen and the logo turned around. "Live" spelled backward was "evil."

Everyone gasped, except Brent.

"Who's Evel?" Brent asked, saying it all wrong, like "level."

"Not Evel," Manny explained. "Evil!"

"I knew it!" Sam slapped her hands together. "Chester's up to something terrible. We have to warn Flint!"

99

"Let's r—" *ZAP!* Earl was frozen.

ZAP! The cheespider was frozen!

The gang was surrounded by the Sentinels of Safety. They had freeze ray guns pointed and ready to fire.

"Run!" Sam made a break for the thickest part of the jungle.

ZAP! Manny's camera was frozen. The camera fell to the ground and shattered.

Manny shed a tear. *ZAP!* He was frozen too.

ZAP! Brent, who was up in the web trying to get his chicken suit on, was also frozen.

Sentinel of Safety Louise smirked, "You're not warning anybody about anything."

The Sentinels of Safety closed in on Sam and Steve.

ZAP! Sam and Steve were frozen.

Barry tried to help Sam, but was held back by the other berries.

Flint's FLFJTPM located the FLDSMDFR. His discovery laser shot through a thicket of jungle, pointing the way. Flint peeked through a bush. In front of them was a towering mountain covered with sparkling rock candy. The mountain's silhouette was the exact shape as the FLDSMDFR, and above it was a swirling mass of rain clouds.

"Water goes in the top, and food comes out the bottom! It's gotta be inside that big rock-candy mountain!" Flint was amazed.

"This is exactly why I wanted you on this mission! Lead on Lockwood!" Chester beamed proudly.

They entered the mountain. In the center, rock candy sparkled like stained glass. With the sun's rays shining through, it looked like a beautiful cathedral of light and color.

Following the FLFJTPM's laser beam, Flint stumbled into the domed space. "The FLDSMDFR must be up there." He pointed at a stone pillar in the middle of the room where a steady waterfall gently poured from above.

Between where they stood and the pillar, there was a deep chasm full of rock-candy stalagmites. Below the pillar, Flint heard the rumbling flow of an underground river.

Chester nervously surveyed the sharp rocks. "A very unpleasant fall. Be careful, Lockwood." He stepped aside so that Flint could lead them across the rock candy.

"Yes, sir." Flint took a few careful hops, starting out across the chasm. It wasn't long before he heaved himself over the edge onto the central pillar. He plopped down into a shallow pool of water. "Made it!" he called back to Chester and Barb.

A noise nearby made Flint turn. He was face to face with his old invention. "Aaaah! FLDSMDFR!" he cried out. The FLDSMDFR's scars had healed with vegetation. Its screen lit up as if to greet an old friend.

Flint whipped out the BSUSB. "Look, I'm sorry to do this to you again. But I can't let your swimming cheespiders escape and attack Lady Liberty. Or the world." As Flint carefully approached the machine to plug in the BSUSB, a marshmallow popped up next to him. The FLDSMDFR's screen projected an image of a marshmallow.

"Marshmallow," the machine said.

An orb of light surged through one of the vines, ending at a pod. The pod swelled, and out plopped a baby marshmallow! Adult marshmallows rushed forward to clean the newcomer.

"Whoa!" Flint tried to understand what he'd just seen. "You're like a family, and you're like their mother?" He stared at his machine while the idea sunk in.

Flint looked at the BSUSB, then back at the marshmallows. "This isn't right." He was about to set aside the BSUSB when Chester appeared behind him.

"There it is! I knew you would lead us to the FLDSMDR," Chester said.

Flint sighed. This was going to be the hardest thing he'd ever said. "I'm starting to think that maybe Sam was right about the food creatures. These marshmallows do seem friendly."

He glanced down. The marshmallows were busy licking Flint's shoes.

"Finish the job, Lockwood," Chester demanded. His eyes were cold and dark.

"No, sir." Flint stepped closer to the FLDSMDFR. It seemed so peaceful. "Chester, I can't do this."

"Fine. I'll do it." Chester snatched the BSUSB

from Flint's hand and put it into the FLDSMDFR. The machine shook violently and a Live Corp logo filled the screen.

"The BSUSB." This wasn't what it was supposed to do. "You reprogrammed it?"

"The machine is what I wanted all along," Chester explained with an evil smile. "And now that I've got what I want, I no longer need you. I'm afraid we're going to have to let you go." Chester shoved Flint over the edge into the abyss below.

"Whaaaat?!" As he fell, the roof of the cavern opened and a Help-icopter dropped a claw to grab the FLDSMDFR, ripping it from its vines.

Suddenly the marshmallows all jumped from their ledges after him. They beat Flint to the bottom and cushioned his fall. Because of them, he landed safely in the river below.

The marshmallows dragged Flint out of the cavern.

The last thing Flint heard was Chester's laughter up above.

CHAPTER 14

Everywhere in the jungle, food creatures were watching their mighty jungle shrivel and disappear. The animals were lost, wandering around confused as their homes faded into dust.

Loud Help-icopters began constructing a giant factory atop the big rock-candy mountain.

Sentinels cleared away chunks of the jungle at the base of the mountain. A leek was sucked up into a container with other food animals and placed on a cargo truck.

Tim and the pickles roasted sardines next to a bonfire. They sat close together, like old friends.

"And then they just left me on the boat," Tim finished his story.

The pickles munched on the sardines they'd caught earlier, listening attentively.

"Hey, you little guys really like sardines, eh?" Tim smiled. "Yeah, this is my kinda place."

Tim's smile turned into a wide grin as he watched a baby pickle cuddled by its happy mom and dad pickles.

"Boy, are they cute at that age," Tim remarked. "But then they grow up and become inventors. That's when things get complicated."

A loud noise made several pickles rush to the river's edge. The pickles worked together to pull a marshmallow man from the river.

The marshmallows leapt off the man, revealing Flint. "Dad?" He was happy to see Tim.

"Flint?!" Tim was surprised.

The marshmallows and pickles greeted each other with "N-woo!" and "Gurgle gurgle."

Before Flint and Tim could say more, the island plants around them began to wither and die.

"Flint, what's happening?" Tim asked. The pickles were panicking.

"Sam's never going to forgive me," Flint said sadly. He knew what was going wrong, and it was all his fault.

The pickles wailed at the sight of the shriveled plants around them.

Flint was distraught.

Tim consoled his new friends. "No, no. Don't cry. Everything's gonna be okay."

Flint held back tears. "No, Dad. It won't be okay! Don't you see? This island's dying without the FLDSMDFR. I really screwed up."

"C'mon, Flint. You'll be able to do something! Look, you've got brains, you've got a lot of talent." Tim added, "You've got a little something stuck to your pants."

A strawberry was hugging Flint's leg.

"Barry!" Flint picked him up.

"N-woo!" Barry said.

"Oh, Barry! I'm so sorry. I really should have listened to Sam," Flint apologized.

"Saspa! Saspa!" Barry said.

"What is it, Barry? What are you trying to say?"

Flint was patient while Barry dressed other strawberries to resemble Sam and the gang. "Saspa! Saspa!" Barry said.

Tim scratched his head while trying to guess. "Sassy pants!"

Barry shook his head.

"Sam and gang!" Flint got it.

"Uh-huh! Uh-huh!" Barry hopped into an orange motorcycle helmet. He picked up a flashlight. Another clue.

"Oh! Looks like a Sentinel of Safety!" Flint guessed.

Barry nodded and started marching around. He poked at the other strawberries, prodding them into a trash can and trapping them.

"They got trashed! They all got trashed." Tim kept trying to figure it out.

"No, Dad," Flint said. "He's saying Sentinels of Safety captured Sam and the gang. We've got to get them out of there."

Flint felt hopeless, but Barry was determined. He

rushed up a near cheese pile to the top of the island's sardine statue. He yodeled, *"Nnnnn-wooooo!"*

"N-woo" echoed back from the wild as the food animals responded. Suddenly food animals converged on Pickle Village.

"N-woooo! N-woooo!" the food animals cried.

"N-wooooooooooooooooooooo!" a tacodile howled.

"What's with all of the 'N-woos'?" Tim asked.

From among the herd of animals, the Remote-Control TV stepped forward.

"Why do they have my TV?" Tim asked as the set turned on.

The TV's static-filled screen showed Flint explaining the FLDSMDFR.

"Water goes in the top and food comes out the bottom!" Flint said to the camera.

The broken video glitched on Flint's name. It repeated the "nnn" from Flint and the "wooo" from Lockwood.

"N-wooooo! N-wooooo!" The food animals recited.

"What's it broken or somethin'? What's it doing?" Tim asked Flint.

109

Flint thought about the foodimals they'd met. Barry. Marshmallows. They'd all called *N-woo*. "It's saying that I'm N-woo! They must think that because I made the FLDSMDFR that makes me their father!"

The food looked at Flint with hope.

Tim gave Flint a big bear hug and said, "I think they've come here for you. See, we all want to help. You should let us."

Flint took a deep breath and hugged his dad harder. He then stepped up next to the sardine statue to give a speech.

"I don't know if you can understand me . . ."

The food creatures stared at him. Barry got on the statue and began translating his words and actions into food speak.

"I know you think I'm N-woo. But the truth is, I'm not N-woo. I'm just a man. A man who's made a lot of mistakes in the last couple days."

Barry said, "Dabba woo ba doo."

Flint went on. "I let myself be used by Chester V and you all are paying the price for that."

"Debba-debba-die!" Barry said.

Tim hugged his pickles close.

"But if there's one thing I've learned, it's that food is people too!" Flint raised his arms in triumph.

"Deeba-dooba-dooba-dee . . ." Barry repeated.

"All of you!" Flint pointed to the crowd.

"Beed-beeda-bodda-boo!" Barry told them.

"Fruits!" Flint shouted.

"Foo!" Barry said, and the fruits cheered.

"Vegetables!"

"Beeja-bow!"

The vegetables shouted.

"And meat!"

"Ann . . . bee!" Barry translated.

The meat products went wild.

"Chester used me. He's using my friends. And I'm pretty sure he wants to use all of you. But I'm not going to let him!"

Barry repeated Flint's charge. "Debba-debba-die!"

"I'm going to break into that factory, get our home back, and save our friends!" Flint finished his speech with flair.

"Deeba-deeba-dens! Ba-dens!" Barry finished too.

111

Then the watermelophants trumpeted. The fruit-cockatiel chirped. The hippotatomus clapped.

Flint, Tim, and Barry looked at the factory being built on the big rock-candy mountain.

The speech was great, but inside Flint was scared. "Okay. How the heck am I going to get in there?"

Tim said, "Flint, with the right rod and tackle, I could get you up there."

"Dad." Flint put his arm around Tim's shoulder and together they said, "Let's go fishing!"

Everyone worked together.

The pickles lassoed the sardine statue, pulling it to the ground.

Shrimpanzees used their fists to pound in metal screws.

A watermelophant pressed its trunk into the bow of Tim's boat. *Splash!* The boat plopped into the water. Tim's boat had been transformed into a floating catapult. The sardine statue rested on the deck. Flint and Barry popped up from the inside of the statue. They nodded at each other.

"Ready, Dad?" Flint shouted.

"Ready, skipper!" Tim answered. Tim grabbed a lever on the boat's control panel. "Catch the big one, buddy." Tim pulled the lever, and the sardine statue was ready to fly. "One, two, and three!"

Flint and Barry soared through the air toward the factory.

"Yesssssssssss!" Flint cheered.

The sardine statue landed perfectly at the top of the factory. Flint and Barry crept out and snuck down a tunnel.

"They could be anywhere in here . . ." Flint noticed a sentinel guarding some cages.

Barry rushed toward the guard. "Saspa?"

The sentinel raised his weapon.

"Hey. How'd you get out—" The sentinel was hit by a huge glob of Barry's jam. "Aaaah! I'm jammed!"

"Good work, Barry!" Flint ran up to a secured glass cage. He saw Sam's backpack and Manny's headset.

"They were here," Flint whispered.

Barry stood next to Flint, punching in a code on a secured door. Barry opened the door and tugged at something. It was the cheespider!

"Aaaaaah! Cheespider!" Flint shouted. "Let's get out of here."

Barry shook his berry head, letting Flint know the cheespider wasn't dangerous. Barry and the cheespider had a quick conversation. Then Barry turned to Flint and said, "Saspa!" He pointed to the right, and then mimed an elevator going down.

"Awesome! Thank you, cheespider," Flint said.

Flint told the strawberry, "Barry, you free the rest of your friends, and I'll go free mine."

Flint rushed out of the elevator. He arrived on the main floor of the factory. Chester and Barb were standing by a console in front of him.

"Lockwood! You're still alive?" Chester asked in amazement.

"That's right," Flint answered.

Flint pulled out two cans of Spray-On Shoes and pointed them at Chester. "Hands up!" he shouted. "Unless you want your face holes sealed forever with Spray-On Shoe! Give me back my friends!"

Chester smiled. "Of course." He turned to Barb. "Monkey," he said, "flip the switch."

Barb flinched at being called a monkey, but flipped a switch and a door in the ceiling opened, revealing Sam, Steve, Earl, Brent, and Manny.

His friends were dangling in the center of a huge darkened room. They were tied up with yellow police tape. Spotlights shone on each person.

"Hey, Flint," Sam said.

Chester and Barb's laughter echoed through the chamber. "I thought you might return," Chester said. "And I knew just who you'd be looking for."

Flint pointed to his two cans of Spray-On Shoes. "Let them go, Chester!"

"Oh, I'll let them go." Chester pressed a button on a remote control device. "Right into my super-sized food-bar machine!"

"Food bars? You're going to turn them into food bars?" Flint shouted.

Chester smiled smugly.

"Since you're all about to die—as I can't leave any witnesses—I don't mind letting you in on a little secret."

Chested pointed up to a higher catwalk and a giant containment tank.

"I needed your invention to keep Live Corp afloat. Innovate or die, Lockwood."

Chester pressed a button and lights illuminated the FLDSMDFR submerged in the tank.

"FLDSMDFR!" Flint gasped.

Chester hit another button. The FLDSMDFR displayed a watermelon on its screen.

"Watermelon," the FLDSMDFR announced.

The FLDSMDRF rattled and a pile of baby watermelophants plopped into a jar.

"You're a monster!" Sam shouted. "Those are living creatures!"

"Yes, that's the problem," Chester agreed. "Food with legs is much harder to catch. They hide. They fight back. They want to live. Too messy. But now that I control your FLDSMDRF, I can create an unlimited supply of food. All that's left to do is mass-produce my greatest product yet . . . Food Bar version 8.0!"

Flint shook his head. "I never should have believed in you."

"Yes, that was quite foolish," Chester replied.

"Now, if you want your friends back, I suggest you drop your cans."

"Don't do it, Flint! Save the island!" Sam shouted.

"But you are my island!" Flint said to Sam.

"Ewww," Chester gagged at Flint's romantic senti-ment. "Okay, first—*shut up!* Then drop the cans!" He pushed a button on the remote control and the gang began descending toward the food-bar machine.

"Okay, okay." Flint set down his cans.

"Empty your pockets!" Chester didn't trust him.

Flint emptied his pockets: cans, jars, tools, the Celebrationator—it took a few minutes to get it all out. "There!" Flint said at last. "That's everything. Now, let them go!"

"Actually, I changed my mind." Chester made the friends fall faster.

"Fliiiint!" Sam shrieked.

Flint lunged for the remote control but missed.

Chester laughed and split into holograms. Each Chester held the exact same remote control. They danced around Flint.

Leaping at the nearest Chester, Flint tried to swipe

the controller, but his hand went right through. Flint then jumped for another Chester. This time he punched a hologram. He tried another . . . hologram! And another . . . hologram!

"Is it me?" one Chester asked.

"Or me?" another Chester asked.

"Or me?" the third Chester teased.

Flint's friends were now getting closer to the grinding food-bar machine.

Sam struggled to rip the tape. "Earl, can't you break us out of here?"

Earl shook his head. "Yellow police tape—the one thing I can't break."

The real Chester kicked Flint down to the ground.

"Ha-ha-ha!" Chester chuckled. "I win because I'm smart enough to have holograms rather than "friends." Flint racked his brain for a way to save them, but couldn't think of a single idea.

They were doomed.

16

Flint had no clue how to save his friends or the island. He had to admit something important. "My friends are the most important thing in my life. I don't work . . . unless we work together," he told the Chesters.

Sam noticed one of Flint's inventions on the floor close to where he stood.

"Flint! Chester's right. He's won. You should throw him a *party*!" she exclaimed.

"Party?" Flint stared at her, confused.

Understanding finally dawned in Flint's eyes. His Celebrationator!

"Right! I guess it is time to . . . *celebrate*!" Flint peeked over at Steve.

The word "celebrate" echoed in Steve's mind. He broke out of his yellow tape bonds and swung over to the Celebrationator. Steve pressed the button.

"Ceeeeellleeeebrrraaate!" Steve shouted.

The detonating explosion of joy flew through all the holograms, but exposed the real Chester V, covering him with glitter and glue. Flint punched him hard and took the remote.

"Thanks, lab partner!" Flint told Steve.

"Helping!" Steve said.

With the remote, Flint lifted his friends to safety. "Guys! I'm so sorry for—"

Before he could finish, Sam cut him off. Sam pointed toward the FLDSMDFR birthing chamber. "Chester!"

The real Chester, covered in glitter, was climbing a ladder up to the higher level. He broke the glass holding the FLDSMDFR and grabbed the machine.

"I've got what I want! Enjoy your friends, Lockwood!" Chester turned to escape down the south catwalk, but the pathway was barred by Barry in a Robo-Suit, standing with all the freed food.

"Besta babba doo doo," Barry said.

Chester flipped around to the north, but that path was blocked by the cheespider.

121

"Raaaaaaaaaaaaar!" The cheespider opened its gaping, ketchup-dripping buns.

Chester took the east catwalk, only to find Earl somersaulting onto the platform to meet him. Earl was followed by Manny and Brent.

Manny was riding a tacodile. "Tacodile supreme!" he shouted.

"Uh-oh!" Brent said.

Panicked, Chester turned west, only to find Flint, Sam, and Steve blocking his way.

"Hate to rain on your parade but—" Sam started.

"—you're finished, Chester," Flint ended.

"Steve!" Steve said.

Completely surrounded, Chester climbed on top of the birthing chamber. Something caught his eye from above. Barb came swinging in like Tarzan.

"Good monkey! Save me!" Chester raised his arms.

"I'm an ape!" Barb said. She snagged the FLDSM-DFR from Chester and swung away. Chester stretched for it, causing him to lose his balance.

"Noooo!" Chester fell straight toward the grinding machine. The holograms were standing on the catwalk below. "Holograms! Save me!"

The holograms linked arms and legs to form a human net over the mouth of the machine. Chester fell right through them because they were holograms.

"Oh fudge," Chester said. He tucked himself inside his vest like a turtle. The vest bounced inside the food bar machine—*boink!*—and then bounced out. Chester laughed.

"Ha! I saved myself!"

Chester rushed toward an exit, only to meet face-to-face with the Cheespider. The Cheespider shot out a cheese web, grabbing Chester before he could escape. *Chomp!* The cheespider ate Chester in one bite. *Gulp!* Then it spit out his yellow vest.

Sam and Flint looked at each other and said one word at the same time: "Eeew."

"Now that'll leave a bad taste in your mouth," said Manny.

Barb walked over to Flint and handed him the FLDSMDFR. "Uh . . . I believe this belongs to you," she said.

Flint smiled.

Flint placed the FLDSMDFR back into its pool in the big rock-candy mountain.

"Here you go. I hope this works."

For a moment the machine sat silently. Flint held his breath. Was his FLDSMDFR gone forever?

Flint moved back as vines reattached to the FLDSMDFR. Color exploded from the machine, illuminating the big rock-candy mountain in a rainbow of light.

"*Yes!*" Flint cheered.

"Pickles. Strawberry." The FLDSMDFR was back to work. "Cheeseburger."

"Yaaay!" The entire mountain shook with cheers.

The vegetation came back to life, and the island became a place where everyone could live happily together: food, animals, food animals, and people.

"It's over." Sam breathed a big sigh.

"Not quite. There's one last thing I need to do."

Flint turned to his friends. "Sam! Guys! I'm so sorry I put you through all this. I wanted to be like Chester V, but what I needed was you. My friends. I hope we can still . . . you know . . . work together?"

Sam smiled.

"I think we'll all work great together."

Flint and Sam finally had their big kiss.

"I'm proud of you, son," Tim said. "Today you caught the Big One."

"I couldn't have reeled him in without you, Dad," Flint replied.

On top of the big rock-candy mountain, the Remote-Control TV watched over everything. Someone hit play on the VCR strapped to the TV's head. The TV showed a video of the Sparkswood grand-opening celebration.

It was perfect.

It was a delicious dream come true.